Terrible Twin
Mania

by: Jan Fields
Illustrated by: Tracy Bishop

7|14

visit us at www.abdopublishing.com

Published by Magic Wagon, a division of the ABDO Group,
PO Box 398166, Minneapolis, MN 55439. Copyright © 2014 by
Abdo Consulting Group, Inc. International copyrights reserved
in all countries. All rights reserved. No part of this book may
be reproduced in any form without written permission from the
publisher.

Calico Chapter Books™ is a trademark and logo of Magic Wagon.

Printed in the United States of America, North Mankato, Minnesota.
102013
012014

Written by Jan Fields
Illustrated by Tracy Bishop
Edited by Stephanie Hedlund and Rochelle Baltzer
Cover and interior design by Renée LaViolette

Library of Congress Cataloging-in-Publication Data

Fields, Jan, author.
  Terrible twin mania / by Jan Fields ; illustrated by Tracy Bishop.
    pages cm. -- (Meri's mirror)
  Summary: When twins Sean and Sophia from California enroll
in Meri's class she gets off on the wrong foot with Sophia--so she
turns to her magic mirror for help in finding a way to apologize even
though two of the class bullies keep interfering.
  ISBN 978-1-62402-011-7
1. Twins--Juvenile fiction. 2. Magic mirrors--Juvenile fiction.
3. Friendship--Juvenile fiction. 4. Apologizing--Juvenile fiction.
5. Bullying--Juvenile fiction. 6. Elementary schools--Juvenile
fiction. [1. Twins--Fiction. 2. Magic--Fiction. 3. Mirrors--Fiction. 4.
Friendship--Fiction. 5. Apologizing--Fiction. 6. Bullying--Fiction. 7.
Schools--Fiction.] I. Bishop, Tracy, illustrator. II. Title.
  PZ7.F479177Te 2014
  813.6--dc23
                          2013025337

Table of Contents

Go Fish

Meredith Mercer sat on her bed with her pillows piled up behind her and a book in her hand. This was her favorite rainy day place to read.

Now and then, she looked at the old mirror hanging over her desk. Aunt Prudence had sent her the mirror for her birthday. It was magic, a secret only Meri knew. If she left a book on her desk, a character would appear in the mirror.

At first, the mirror was a little scary. No one expects to find a stranger where their face should be! Plus, the mirror only let Meri *see* the character. It didn't let her talk to the character. Meri had solved that with a little practical thinking. She used a gadget that turned any surface into a speaker.

Making friends with book characters was fun. But the character couldn't leave the mirror room while the book was on the desk. The mirror was like a cage. Meri didn't want to do that to her book friends. When she met Anne of Green Gables, they had lots of fun until Anne got homesick. Maybe the answer was to only have short visits.

Meri sighed and looked down at the book she was reading, *A Little Princess*. She knew she'd like chatting with Sarah Crewe. Sarah knew what it was like to be different from the kids at her school.

Sarah liked reading, learning, and imagining. The girls at her school just liked fancy clothes and talking about each other. Then when Sarah's papa died, the owner of the school made Sarah live in the freezing attic and work all day. Meri's house was old and sometimes it got cold in the winter, but she had never been really cold or hungry.

If Meri used her magic mirror, Sarah could tell her one of her wonderful stories. The book was full of Sarah's stories, but Meri wanted to hear them for herself. Meri loved stories.

Meri looked at the mirror again. When she finished reading the book then maybe she would chat with Sarah for a day. She wouldn't make her stay days and days. Meri nodded to herself firmly and dove back into the book.

A few minutes later, her little brother, Thomas, peeked around her doorway. He held up a deck of cards. "Do you want to play Go Fish?"

"Not right now," she said. "I'm reading."

Thomas walked in and leaned over her to look at the book. "That looks boring. Cards are more fun."

Meri closed the book with her finger between the pages to hold her place. "Why don't you go play with Kyle?"

"I'm not allowed. We climbed up on his shed roof and dropped dirt bombs on Mr. Colby's dog."

Meri nodded. "Yep, that would do it. You and Kyle should think these ideas through."

Thomas rolled his eyes. "That wouldn't be much fun."

"Why don't you play with Kat?"

"She only wants to play dolls and dress up. She's such a girl."

"I'm a girl too," Meri said.

"She's worse."

Meredith laughed. "Well, I'm not going to play right now. I'm reading." She looked pointedly at her little brother, waiting for him to leave. Instead, he walked over to poke at her mirror. "How come you don't talk to your mirror anymore?"

"What?" Meri yelped. She'd kept her magic mirror very secret.

"I heard you talking and talking in here, but you don't do it anymore."

"Mom explained that to you," Meredith said carefully. "Remember, about the talking books that I download from the library?"

Thomas looked at her. "I know when I hear *you* talking."

"Maybe it just sounded like me."

Thomas sighed a huge dramatic sigh. "Okay, don't tell me. Nobody tells me anything." He stomped out of the room.

Meredith turned back to her book. For a moment, she just stared at the pages. She thought about what Thomas said.

Thomas might figure out that her mirror was magic. He was smart. And he would tell everyone. She planned to tell her family, someday. But she liked having something that was just hers. In a big family, that didn't happen often. She didn't want her nosy little brother messing it up.

With a sigh of her own, she shook off the worry and turned back to her book.

California Twin Crazy

The next day, Meredith took *A Little Princess* to school with her. She entered her fourth grade classroom and hurried to her seat. She hoped to finish her book during free reading time.

Kaylin and the mean girls looked her way, but they didn't come over. Meri was glad. They didn't pick on her much anymore, but she was still sad about losing Kaylin as a real friend.

As Meri took her seat at the worktable, Jasmine looked up and smiled. "I love Mondays."

Meri laughed. "I do too. That probably makes us a little weird."

Jasmine shrugged. "I like school better than home right now. My mom is teaching Carl how to use the potty. It's not pretty."

"I'm glad Thomas and Kat are way past that," Meri said.

"Oh, that must have been terrible," Jasmine said. "Two times as many diapers, accidents, and smell!" She waved a hand in front of her face as if the smell was around them.

"Twins add two times as much of everything," Meri said.

Just then, Mrs. Miller walked into the classroom followed by two students Meri had never seen before. They both had thick, shiny black hair and skin the color of toffee. The girl was a little taller than the boy. But both had the same big, dark eyes and sharp chins.

Mrs. Miller clapped her hands for attention. "Today, we welcome two new friends to Room Eight," she said. "This is

Sean and Sonia Wilson. They moved here from California. Please give them a warm Connecticut welcome."

"Wow, twins! They look amazing," Jasmine said softly.

Meri thought so too, but suddenly she didn't want to say it. "I guess," she said instead. She watched as Kaylin's group rushed to claim the new students. "I'd love to sit with you," Sonia said, smiling as they towed her to their table.

Sean waved off the girls. "Thanks, but I think I'd like to sit back there." He pointed at the table farthest from the front where David, Blake, and Steve sat. He headed straight back to the table. The guys all exchanged high fives before Sean settled into a seat. Meri wondered what it was like to be so sure that strangers would like you right away.

Mrs. Miller beamed at the class, as if they'd all done something really great. Meri wasn't sure why everyone thought the new twins were a big deal. Jasmine stared at the new girl like she was a movie star. The girl waved her hands around as she talked to the mean girls. Meri shook her head. They were just two new kids. Why all the fuss?

Meri bent over her morning work so that she couldn't see either of the twins anymore. She hoped everything would settle down soon. Meri didn't like change. Sometimes change was good, but sometimes it was bad. She didn't like to take the risk. And the new twins brought a big rush of change into Meri's class.

During circle time, Mrs. Miller let everyone ask the twins questions. Meri squirmed as she watched Kaylin grin and nudge Sonia. Then Meri turned to whisper to Jasmine, but Jasmine's attention was fixed on Sonia. Meri finally sat back and crossed her arms.

"Did you know any movie stars?" Kaylin asked. Meri was sure she only asked the question so Sonia could show off.

"I've seen lots of stars at restaurants," Sonia said. "And Pip Gregory went to our school

until he got a role on *Mission: Space Camp.*
Now he has classes right at the TV studio.
Sean spent a day on set with him once."

"I would go back," Sean said with a grin.
"But I was banned. It had something to do with
marshmallows in the tofu chili and toothpaste
in the cupcake icing on the food service table."

While the kids laughed, Mrs. Miller's
cheerful smile slipped a little. "We don't

appreciate those kinds of pranks here," she said sternly. "Especially since eating toothpaste can be dangerous."

"Of course," Sean said seriously. "I learned my lesson about pranks."

Meri recognized Sean's innocent expression. It was the same one she often saw on her brother's face after he cooked up some plan with Kyle. She hoped Mrs. Miller wasn't fooled.

Meri checked her lunch carefully when Mrs. Miller announced it was lunchtime. She hadn't seen Sean go into the coatroom, but you had to be careful with a prankster around.

"Do you think we could scoot closer to Sonia's table?" Jasmine asked.

Meri turned shocked eyes toward her. "She's sitting at the mean girl table."

"I know. We don't have to sit with them," Jasmine said. "I just want to be a little closer. Then I can hear Sonia. She might be talking about movie stars."

Meri began unwrapping her sandwich. "She only knows that one boy."

"Pip Gregory," Jasmine said. "He's cute."

Meri stared at her again. Jasmine never talked about boys being cute. This was a change Meri definitely did not like.

"You can scoot closer if you want," Meri said. "I'll stay here. I can read while I eat."

"Okay, great!" Jasmine scooted her chair close to the mean girl table. To Meri's surprise, the mean girls didn't seem to notice. Almost all the girls had scooted closer to Sonia. Meri shook her head and bit into her sandwich.

Even if all of Room Eight went California twin crazy, she was going to stay right where she was.

As Meri unwrapped her sandwich, she thought again about *A Little Princess*. When Sarah started at her boarding school, everyone made a big fuss over her. But Sarah didn't soak up the attention like Sonia. Sarah was different. Meri was sure of that.

Meri's Jealous

After lunch, the girls left the room in a parade led by Sonia. As they passed Meri's table, Jasmine whispered, "Aren't you coming out to the playground? Sonia is going to tell us more about California."

Meri shook her head.

"Don't you even want to meet Sonia and Sean?" Jasmine asked.

"I have twins at home," she said. "It's not a big deal."

Jasmine looked confused. Then she shrugged and hurried to catch up to the parade. Meri opened *A Little Princess*. Soon her attention drifted to the table near the back of the room. The boys were usually the first the first ones out of the room. Sean was whispering to the other boys. Meri doubted he was talking about movie stars. He was probably cooking up trouble.

When the boys turned to look in her direction, Meri quickly dropped her eyes to her book. The boys were up to something. Meri glanced over at Mrs. Miller's desk. Her teacher was staring into her computer screen and tapping keys.

Finally, Mrs. Miller stood up. She looked toward the table full of boys in surprise. "Aren't you guys going out to play?" she asked.

"Oh, yeah," Sean said. "Right now. I love recess."

The group nearly fell over one another as they headed for the door. Mrs. Miller watched them with a small frown on her face. Finally she looked over at Meri with a smile. "I need to go speak to the librarian. Will you be okay in here alone?"

Meri nodded and held up her book. "I'm trying to finish this."

Mrs. Miller's smile grew as she saw the cover. "I really liked that book when I was a girl. Is it your first time reading it?"

Meri nodded. "I like Sarah Crewe."

"I'm not surprised. She reminds me a little of you. Sometimes she liked to be alone, too. Well, I'll be back in a few minutes."

Mrs. Miller hurried out of the room. Meri thought what she said was strange. Sarah was an only child. Meri had a house full of sisters and a wild little brother. Sarah told stories that made everyone listen. Meri thought she and Sarah were mostly very different.

While she was staring down at the book and thinking about it, she caught movement out of the corner of her eye. She looked toward the door but didn't see anyone. She shrugged and turned back to the story, looking for ways she was like Sarah Crewe as she read.

She was soon caught up in Sarah's misery in the attic. Miss Minchin had taken all of Sarah's beautiful things. She even took Sarah's books! Meri was almost sure she would have complained a lot more than Sarah did.

Meri jumped when the class began pouring into the room. Meri frowned at the Sonia parade again.

Finally, Jasmine slipped back into the chair beside Meri. "I would love to live in California," she said. "Can you imagine going out to supper and seeing someone famous at the next table? It's so exciting to think about."

Jasmine leaned forward on her elbows. "I'm so glad Sonia is in our class," she said in a dreamy voice. "You should have been outside. All the kids from the other classes wanted to hear Sonia's stories, too. And all the boys wanted to play with Sean."

"How can you be sure Sonia isn't making those stories up?" Meri asked.

"Why would she?"

"To get everyone's attention," Meri said. "To get everyone to follow her around like little ducks behind their mama."

"Sounds like you're just jealous!"

Meri turned sharply to see Sonia standing near their table. She held a dull pencil in her hand and had her arms crossed. Jasmine gasped.

"I'm not jealous," Meri said. "I just don't think you're a big deal."

"I never said I was a big deal," Sonia said. "I don't make people listen to my stories. They asked. They're being nice. You should try that sometime." Then she turned sharply and stormed over to the pencil sharpener, muttering about "mean girls."

Meri blinked and looked after her. "I'm not a mean girl."

"Today you are," Jasmine said, "a little."

"Whose side are you on?"

"The side that thinks you're acting strange," Jasmine said. "You're usually so nice. Sonia didn't do anything wrong."

Meri knew Jasmine was right. Sonia hadn't done anything wrong, except maybe show off a little. Meri knew it wasn't wrong to be the new girl or to have interesting stories. Sarah Crewe had those things, and Meri liked her. So why did Meri feel so angry about the twins?

She was glad when Mrs. Miller called everyone's attention to the front of the room.

She didn't want to think about the twins anymore.

Everything felt normal for a while, until it was time for reading groups. The class moved around, gathering into the groups for their reading level. Mrs. Miller called Sonia and Sean to the front of the room to have them read with her so she would know what group they should be in. Meri just hoped neither one would end up in her group.

David had stayed in his usual seat. So Meri and Jasmine walked over to join him for their group.

"We need to pick a new book," Meri said.

"Anything's fine," David said. "As long as it's not too girly." He pointed at the book in Meri's hand. "And as long as it doesn't have the word *princess* in the title."

Meri smiled. "I wasn't going to suggest this one. I'm reading it for fun. It's about a rich girl who ends up being really poor. All the kids and teachers at her school are mean to her because she's poor. She has to live in a freezing attic and work hard and she doesn't get enough food."

"You have weird ideas about reading for fun," David said.

"Maybe we could read something about California," Jasmine suggested.

"That could be good," David said. "We should ask Mrs. Miller if she has books like that."

"I think she's busy," Meri said, looking toward the front where the twins were reading. She saw Mrs. Miller nod toward their table. Sonia looked upset and shook her head. Mrs. Miller looked at Meri and their eyes met. Meri thought Mrs. Miller looked confused.

David tapped Meri on the arm, drawing her attention back to him. "What's the matter?"

"Nothing," Meri said.

"You sound mad."

"Meri's jealous of the twins," Jasmine whispered.

Meri looked at Jasmine, her eyes wide in shock. "I am not. I can't believe you said that."

"What do you call it then?" Jasmine asked. "You don't like them, and you don't even know them."

"They're show-offs," Meri muttered.

"Sean's not," David said. "He's really cool and funny. And he has great ideas. You didn't even talk to him."

"She didn't talk to Sonia either," Jasmine said. "Sonia's really nice, and she tells great stories about California."

"Hey!" Meri said. "I thought you two were my friends."

"We are," Jasmine said. "But if friends don't tell you the truth, who will?"

Meredith glared at both of them. "Can we just pick a book, please?"

David shrugged and Jasmine sighed. Then the three of them got up and walked to the reading group bins in silence.

Sarah Crewe

Meri was glad when the horrible day was over. She was pretty sure she'd lost her two best friends to the terrible twins. Her class was totally twin crazy. She wished she could just stay home until everyone got over it.

She hauled her backpack up to her room and dropped it on her bed. She had a math worksheet and her reading log for homework. She pulled out the worksheet and sat at her desk to work on it. Usually she zipped through her worksheets, but thoughts of the day kept pushing into her head. It made it hard to remember her math facts.

Finally, she sighed and looked up at herself in the mirror. Her round, pale face and poof of crazy blonde curls looked back at her. She looked a little ghostly in the smoky glass of the old mirror.

"I'm not jealous," she told her reflection. Her mirror image didn't have anything to say.

Meri looked over at her backpack. She could really use someone to talk to. Finally she got up and pulled *A Little Princess* from the backpack. She carefully placed the book in the exact middle of her desk. Then she plugged in the gadget that turned her mirror into a speaker.

She looked into the mirror at her own image again. "See you later, Meri," she said. She carried her math worksheet over to her bed and used her backpack as a table while she worked the rest of the problems. She didn't let herself peek at the mirror until she was done.

Finally she stuffed the finished worksheet into her backpack. She took a deep breath and looked quickly into the mirror.

The girl who stared back at her no longer had a round face or blonde curls. Instead she had short, heavy black hair that curled at the tips. She had big greenish-gray eyes and long dark lashes. She was thin and slightly taller than Meri. Her dress was worn and a bit small.

"Sarah Crewe," Meredith whispered.

Sarah looked surprised, but she merely said, "I am. What is your name?"

"Meredith Mercer, but everyone calls me Meri."

"How very pretty," Sarah said. "Like the name of an especially lovely doll."

"I wish I could see your doll Emily," Meri said.

Sarah turned to look around the room. It was a mirror version of Meredith's room with its narrow bed piled with handmade quilts and its long bookcase packed with Meri's books.

"I don't have Emily here," Sarah said. She smiled a small, dreamy smile. "Perhaps she has gone out for a walk. I had to go to the shops this morning for Miss Minchin and it was very cold and wet. But maybe it has turned lovely, and Emily is out walking."

Meri nodded. "It's sunny, but a little cool."

"Oh, I do hope Emily has worn her cloak," Sarah said. "Perhaps she has taken a penny with her to buy a nice warm bun. A warm bun is lovely on a cool day."

"Does Emily have many adventures?" Meri asked as she slipped into her desk chair.

"Yes," answered Sara. "At least I believe she does. At least I pretend I believe she does. And that makes it seem as if it were true. Do you like to pretend things?"

"Sometimes," Meri said. "I like stories."

"I love stories, especially about the French Revolution," Sarah said. "I like Marie Antoinette. She was very brave even when she was thrown in prison. I think about her sometimes when I am trying to sleep on my hard bed and I am very cold."

"I don't know a lot about her," Meri said.

"I can tell you about her," Sarah said, her gray-green eyes bright. "Or help you with your French lessons, if you like. I help Ermengarde. She's my friend, too."

"I don't take French lessons," Meri said. "But I do have something I'd like to tell you about."

Sarah sat in the chair at the desk on her side of the mirror and folded her hands neatly into her lap. "Please," she said, "tell me whatever you like. I promise to listen closely."

"There are two new students at my school," Meri said. "They are twins. And everyone is crazy about them. They watch everything the twins do and act like they're super special. But they're just kids."

"Kids?" Sarah said in alarm. "You have baby goats at your school? That must be funny."

Meredith laughed as she pictured Sonia as a goat. "No, they're children—a brother and sister. *Kids* means 'children' around here."

"Oh," Sarah said. "What a strange thing to call children."

"I guess it is. I never thought about it," Meri admitted. "Anyway, the problem is that Sonia and Sean are not that special. I don't know why everyone is acting like they are."

Sarah nodded, her face serious. "The other girls acted that way when I came to the Select Seminary for Young Ladies. I believe it was because Miss Minchin made such a fuss. She smiled at me, but she didn't like me a bit. The other girls didn't know what to think about me. Some were nice, but some were jealous."

Meri folded her arms. "Well, I don't think anyone would be jealous of Sonia."

"Does she have fancy clothes? My papa always gave me so many lovely clothes," Sarah said. "The other girls seemed to like looking at them. I think that is what made Lavinia jealous. Lavinia was quite unpleasant when I joined the school," Sarah sighed. "She still is."

"Well, Sonia does dress different,"

Meri said. "I think it's because she's from California."

"California!" Sarah's eyes opened wide. "That's so far away. I can't imagine ever going to America. Do they still have cowboys there? I think that knowing cowboys would be exciting."

Meri felt her stomach knot. Would Sarah act just like everyone else because the twins were from California? "I don't see what's so exciting about California."

"It's so far away," Sarah said. "It's like a dream, but you know it's a real place." Then Sarah opened her eyes wide as if she just had a surprising thought. "Maybe that is why the other girls liked me at first. India was like a dream for them, and I had lived there."

Meri guessed California was a little like a dream. Everyone knew about it because of movie stars, but you didn't expect to meet people from there. When Sonia and Sean had told all their California stories, would they be just regular kids in the class?

5

A Decision

"Maybe that is why everyone likes them," Meri said. "Maybe they won't like them forever."

"That is probably true. Now that I live in the attic, no one seems to be jealous of me. Although, Lavinia is still unkind," Sarah said. "Are the twins nice?"

"I guess, sometimes," Meri said. "Sonia said she thought I was jealous of her. That's not very nice."

"Were you nice to her?"

Meri squirmed in her seat. She knew the answer to that and didn't like it.

"Everyone was acting like Sonia was some kind of princess!" Then Meri froze. That's exactly how everyone treated Sarah before things turned so terrible for her in the book.

"That must be embarrassing for Sonia," Sarah said. "It is pleasant to be admired. But when you know that you're really rather plain and ordinary, it feels strange to have so many people acting as if you are special."

"She didn't act embarrassed," Meri grumbled.

"Perhaps she was pretending," Sarah said. "I pretend rather a lot. Sometimes pretending is all I have." Then she leaned forward and whispered. "Only now I don't have to pretend all the time. Someone has been leaving me presents in the attic and they are real. It has made things much better. I do love pretending, but sometimes real is much better."

"I know," Meri said softly, thinking of the terrible things Sarah had to face in the book. Suddenly she felt bad about how she acted around Sonia. She thought of the mean girl in *A Little Princess* and sighed. "I acted like Lavinia."

Sarah looked at her in surprise. "Oh, maybe only a little. You have such kind eyes. I find it hard to imagine Lavinia ever having such kind eyes."

"I don't think my eyes were kind when I looked at Sonia," Meri said.

"Then you know what you must do."

"Apologize?" Meri whispered.

"I should think so," Sarah said. "You must admit your offense and beg pardon for it. I believe you'll be greatly relieved if you do."

Meri nodded. "You're right. I'll apologize to her tomorrow at school."

Sarah smiled. "I am certain I would forgive Lavinia if she apologized. Though I cannot imagine her doing such a thing. I might find it hard. She had been very unkind. When trying to do something difficult, it helps to pretend."

"You mean you would pretend Lavinia is someone else?" Meri asked.

"No, I pretend I am someone else. I pretend I am a princess, so that I can try to behave like one. You might try that," Sarah said, serious again. "It does help when doing difficult things. I often pretend when Miss Minchin or Cook are scolding me."

"I'll try that tomorrow, too," Meri said.

Just then, Meri's mother yelled up the stairs that it was time for everyone to come down to supper. "That's my mom. I have to go," Meri said. "It's suppertime."

"Oh," Sarah's eyes opened wide. "It must be lovely to have a mama and a family to eat with you."

"I wish you could come down and eat with us." Then Meri remembered something. "Oh, look in the bottom drawer of the desk!"

She watched as Sarah bent over and she heard the dragging sound of the drawer opening. "There is a bag in here," Sarah said. "It's made of the strangest slippery fabric."

"Pull it out of the drawer," Meri said. "It's my snack stash. You can have it."

Sarah put the plastic bag on the desktop and looked inside. She pulled out a small package of cookies and looked at them. "They are wrapped in slippery paper and sealed."

"Yes, but you can pull them open," Meri said. "They're good."

"Thank you," Sarah said. "You are as kind

as the person who leaves me mysterious surprises in my attic room."

Meri heard another shout from downstairs. "We're going to eat without you if you don't get down here," her sister Judith bellowed.

"Coming!" Meri shouted back.

"I think princesses do not shout in their houses," Sarah said.

Meri smiled back at her. "I'm new to the princess thing. I have to go, but I'll be back."

When she slipped into her seat at the table, her dad turned to her and raised one eyebrow. "I was starting to wonder if you were skipping supper."

"Not likely," Thomas said. "Mom made meatloaf."

Meredith did like her mother's meatloaf. Her mom smiled at her and passed a plate with a thick slice of meatloaf, a small scoop of her fluffy mashed potatoes, and a bigger scoop of carrots. Her mom always remembered the Meri loved carrots but didn't really like mashed potatoes.

Meri looked down at her plate. She thought about Sarah's supper of cookies and candy and wished she could share the hot food with her. She knew Sarah was really just a character in a book, but seeing her in the mirror and talking with her made Meri feel much worse about Sarah's hungry tummy.

"Is something wrong?" Mom asked. "You didn't snack and ruin your appetite, did you?"

"No," Meri said. "I'm hungry." She cut into the meatloaf with her fork and put a big bite in her mouth. It was delicious. It always was.

Meri looked around the table at her noisy family. She saw Thomas sneaking carrots off his plate and accidentally dropping them on the floor. She smiled when his twin sister Kat caught him and immediately told Mom.

Meredith's oldest sister Hannah launched into a funny story from her basketball practice. Soon the whole table was laughing. Thomas laughed so hard that he snorted milk out his nose, bringing a howl from Judith. "You're so gross!"

Meri chuckled as she turned her full attention back to her food. She felt really lucky to have such a great family. And such a yummy supper.

6

"You're Mean!"

The next day, Meri walked into Room Eight with her shoulders back. She was going to face up to what she'd done wrong and fix it. She couldn't believe how mean she'd been to the new girl. That wasn't like her at all.

Just like yesterday, the girls of the class were clustered around Sonia. Unfortunately, the mean girls spotted Meri first.

"Oh, look who's here," Gina said. "Are you still too good to hang out with the rest of us, Meridip?"

Meri shook her head. "I'm not too good to hang out with you, Gina. I just don't want to."

"Good," Gina said. "Because we don't need a Meridip around anyway."

Meri took a deep breath. A princess didn't get drawn off into silly arguments and name calling. A princess stuck to the job at hand.

"Sonia, could I talk to you?" she asked.

"Why would Sonia want to talk to you," Megan asked, "after the things you said yesterday?"

"Can't Sonia talk for herself?" Meri asked. "Or maybe she's a ventriloquist. Maybe she's just throwing her voice into a couple of empty-headed dolls."

Meri's ex-best friend Kaylin looked at her in shock. "That's not very nice, Meri."

"No, it's not," Sonia said. "I don't think I want to talk to you, Meri. You're mean! We had mean girls at my last school. My mom says it's best to ignore them." Then Sonia turned her back to Meri and all the other girls did, too.

Finally only Jasmine was facing Meri. Her eyes were wide and worried. Meri just turned and walked back to the coatroom to put away

her lunch bag and backpack. She didn't know what to do. How could she apologize if Sonia wouldn't even talk to her?

Meri stomped to her worktable and sat down. Well, if they didn't want to talk to her, she didn't want to talk to them either. She pulled a sheet of paper out of the scrap box and began doodling. She drew a picture of a fancy girl with mean eyes.

"Who's that supposed to be?" Jasmine asked as she slipped into her seat beside Meri.

"Nobody, just a drawing," Meri said between gritted teeth.

"It has the same necklace as Sonia," Jasmine pointed out. "And the same side ponytail. And the same . . ."

"It's just a drawing." Meri crumpled up the paper.

"Why are you acting so weird?" Jasmine asked.

Meri looked up at her. "You know, you can go sit at Sonia's table if you want."

"Actually, I can't," Jasmine said. "There's no room. Plus, I didn't want to. My seat is over here with my friend. If you are still my friend."

Meri still felt a thick, hot ball of anger in her chest. She told herself that Jasmine was being mean. She smoothed out her drawing and began shading in the girl's thick, dark hair.

"Well, you let me know when you decide if we're still friends," Jasmine snapped. She reached out to get a scrap paper of her own. The two girls drew in silence until Mrs. Miller walked to the front of the class to begin the day. Meri felt a surge of relief. At least schoolwork was something she understood.

Meri ate lunch alone again at her table. The girls crowded around Sonia. They seemed happy to perch anywhere as long as they could hear the new girl talk.

As Meri chewed her sandwich, she wondered if Sonia was like Sarah Crewe. Maybe she told such good stories that everyone just wanted to listen. Meri wished she could scoot closer to hear, but she didn't want to be called names again.

Finally she wrapped up the rest of her sandwich and tossed it in the trash on her way out of the room. She decided to go outside for recess. Being in the classroom just made her feel bad.

As she stepped out the back door, she blinked at the bright midday sun. With her pale skin, she burned fast in the sun. She considered turning around and going back inside after all.

"Hey, Meri!"

She squinted against the glare and saw David waving her over. "Come on," he yelled. "We're playing kickball. You can make our teams even."

Meri took an uncertain step forward. She didn't really like kickball. Still, it was nice to have someone who wanted to play with her. She took another couple of steps, then she heard Sean.

"Maybe it would be better if she didn't," he said.

"What are you talking about?" David asked. "Meri's my friend."

"Yeah, but she was kind of mean to my sister," Sean said. "Sonia can be a pain sometimes, but she's still my sister."

Meri felt the empty spot inside her stomach turn cold even in the warmth of the sun. "I know I was mean," she said. "I wanted to apologize this morning, but I didn't get a chance."

Sean shrugged. "Maybe you should try again."

"But I still think she can play kickball if she wants," David said firmly.

"It's okay," Meri said. "I don't really like kickball that much. I just wanted to say thanks for asking. Thanks."

"Okay," David said hesitantly. "But you know you can play if you want."

Meri just smiled at him. Then she walked over to the big maple tree in the middle of the playground and sat down to wait for recess to be over.

Don't Know What They're Missing!

As soon as she got home, Meri trudged upstairs and dumped her backpack on her bed. Sarah sat at the mirror desk reading, but she looked up when Meri came in.

"Oh, I'm so glad you've come home," she said. "I've imagined all day how your talk with Sonia might have gone."

"It wasn't very good," Meri said sadly. "I didn't get a chance to apologize at all."

"Why not?" Sarah asked.

"Well, one of the girls she spends time with started saying mean things to me," Meri said. "Then another mean girl joined in. They made fun of my name. When I asked to talk to Sonia, she wouldn't even come and talk to me."

"What did you do about that?" Sarah asked.

"I guess I didn't act like a princess. I wanted to, but I didn't. I acted mean right back at them. It was so hard to do the right thing when Gina and Megan were being so mean."

"That does sound difficult," Sarah agreed. "But it is when you have trials that you learn what kind of child you are. If you have everything you want and everyone is kind to you, how can you find out whether you really are a nice child or a horrible one?"

"So I guess this trial proved it," Meri said. "I'm a horrible, hateful child."

Sarah looked at her for a long quiet moment. Meredith almost felt as if Sarah could look right inside her. Finally, Sarah said, "No, I don't think so. If you were a horrible, hateful child, you wouldn't care at all about making up with Sonia. You wouldn't mind being horrible. You'd be glad. When Lavinia is mean, she is glad. I can see it on her face. But you want to do good. I think that is in your favor."

Meri wasn't sure she followed all that, but she was glad Sarah didn't think she was an awful person. "What should I do?"

"What do you think you should do?" Sarah asked her.

Meri sighed. "I should try again to apologize. Maybe I could write it down. Then when Sonia sees my apology on a card, she might let me say it to her in person."

"I think that is a wonderful idea," Sarah said. "Would you like me to read it?"

"That would be nice of you," Meri said. "And I think I'll draw some flowers on the card. I'm good at drawing flowers."

"That's good. Everything looks better with flowers. And maybe a little bird. I have birds that are my friends in the attic. They're only small and not very colorful, but in a drawing you can make them look however you like."

Meri bent over the paper to begin her card. She felt better than she had all day. Suddenly she looked up into Sarah's green-gray eyes. "It's good to have a friend."

"Nothing is ever quite as bad or quite as lonely when you have a friend," Sarah agreed.

Meredith wrote that she was sorry for not welcoming Sonia to class. She admitted she had acted like a mean girl but didn't want to be a mean girl at all. And she said she was sure that Sonia's California stories were exciting.

Sarah looked over the note when Meri pressed it to the mirror. "You only need one 't' in admit," she said. "And the end sounds a little like you're asking her to tell you a story."

"I do want to hear them," Meri said. "I saw her telling stories today and I thought that she might be like you. You tell great stories. I can't do that, but I love stories."

"I do too," Sarah agreed. "But you must remember to be nice, even if she won't tell you her stories."

Meri folded her paper to make the outside of the card and began drawing flowers and a bird. She held the picture up often, so Sarah could give suggestions about colors or the best way for the bird to look friendly.

She had barely finished when her dad called her for supper. "Oh, I'll have to do my homework after supper," she said. Time had slipped away much quicker than she expected.

"Maybe I could help," Sarah suggested. She looked so eager that Meri suddenly wondered if Sarah was lonely.

"Is it terrible," Meri asked, "being in the mirror when I'm at school or supper?"

"I do wish I could go with you," Sarah said. "But it's not terrible. No one makes me go out in the freezing streets. And I haven't felt a bit hungry since you showed me the bag of treats."

"Do tell me if it gets too lonely," Meri said. "I can take the book away, and I think you'll go home."

Sarah laughed, though it didn't sound very happy. "You mean back to Miss Minchin's school? That's not really home, though my attic is not so very terrible since my secret friend has been leaving dinner for me." Then her eyes grew round. "Was that you? Did you use magic to do that, like you did for this mirror?"

Meri shook her head. "No, but when you go back you'll find out who it really is. I promise."

"Do you think so?" Sarah asked. "Is seeing my future a part of your magic mirror?"

Meri shook her head. "No, I can't see the future in the mirror. I saw it in the book, and I know it's true. I have to go now though. I'll get in trouble if they have to yell for me twice every night."

Sarah smiled as she shook her head. "I still do not think a royal family shouts back and forth in the palace."

"Then they don't know what they're missing," Meri said.

Easier than a Shark Bite

Meri ran into Room Eight the next morning. She wanted to hand her card to Sonia before she chickened out. If everyone in her whole class thought Sonia was interesting, Meri wanted a chance to get to know her, too.

To her surprise, Sonia wasn't surrounded by all the girls in class. Instead, she sat in her chair working on the math sheet from the night before. Kaylin sat beside her, pointing to different word problems on the paper.

Meri thought the math sheet was hard, too. She wasn't sure she would have gotten all the answers without Sarah's help after supper. Sarah had loved the word problems and sometimes wanted to make up whole stories to go with them. Still, she was a big help when Meri pulled her attention back to the math part of the story problems.

Meri wove through the classroom tables and noticed that more than one person was desperately working on the same sheet. She was almost to Sonia when someone reached around from behind her and snatched the card from her hand.

"How sweet," Gina said. "Meri's been drawing birdies."

"Tweet, tweet," Megan squeaked.

"Give it back, Gina," Meri said, snatching at the card.

Instead, the taller girl held it over Meri's head. Meri jumped to grab the paper, hoping Mrs. Miller came in to stop Gina's teasing.

"Just give it to her," Kaylin said.

Sonia looked up from her paper, frowned at Meri, then said, "I'm trying to work. Give her the paper back."

At the sound of Sonia's voice, Gina turned slightly and Meri was able to snag the edge of the card. She pulled. Gina jerked hard on the other end. The card ripped right down the middle.

"Gina!" Kaylin and Sonia said at the same moment.

Meri looked at the torn half of the card in her hand.

"Oops," Gina said. "Well, I guess it's just trash now." She crumpled her half of the card and tossed it into the classroom trash. Meri sighed and walked to the trash can. She threw her own half in and walked to her desk as Mrs. Miller walked in the room.

Mrs. Miller took one look at Meri's face and said, "What's wrong?"

"I'm okay," Meri said as she slumped into her chair. How was she going to apologize now? She couldn't get Sonia to listen to her. The note she'd worked on for so long was nothing but trash now. Meri sighed as Mrs. Miller clapped her hands to call for attention.

"We're not going to have a morning work packet today," she said. "Instead, we're going to do a writing practice. So get out a fresh sheet of paper, and get ready to write!"

Meri pulled out a sheet of lined paper. She hoped the writing prompt wouldn't be anything funny or happy. She didn't feel like she could do a good job on anything like that.

Mrs. Miller looked around the room to be sure everyone had a paper and pencil ready. "We're going to write a story from your life. I want you to write about the hardest thing you've ever done and what you learned from doing it. Okay, go!"

Meri stared down at her blank page. She thought about how much trouble she was having just saying "sorry" to Sonia. She knew she'd done hard things before, but that felt like the hardest thing of all—especially since she hadn't managed to do it yet. Meri's pencil flew along the page as she poured out all her feelings about the last few days.

Finally Mrs. Miller called for everyone to stop writing and pass their papers to the front. Meri looked down at her page full of words. She realized that she felt a little better just from writing about how hard the last few days had been.

The rest of the morning went quickly. When lunch came, Meri went out to sit under the tree again. It seemed like the easiest way to stay out of trouble. She noticed that some of the other girls came outside, too. She was surprised when Jasmine pushed open the door and ran out to sit with Meri.

"I thought you'd be listening to Sonia," Meri said.

"Sonia is nice," Jasmine said. "But it's not much fun to be around Gina and Megan. I think even Kaylin gets tired of them."

Meri remembered Kaylin and Sonia snapping at Gina for tearing up the card. "They didn't like it when Gina tore up my card," she said.

Jasmine nodded, and they sat quietly for a few minutes. Finally, Jasmine asked, "What was in that card this morning?"

"It was for Sonia," Meri said. "I was apologizing for being mean."

Jasmine smiled brightly. "That's nice."

Meri shrugged. "It didn't help. She didn't get to see it."

"You should make another one."

"It's too easy for Gina to tear it up," Meri said. "I guess she'll just be mad at me forever. I wish I heard at least one California story."

"I could tell you one," Jasmine said. "I remember some of them."

Meri knew it wouldn't be the same, but she listened anyway. Jasmine did have a good memory, though it sounded strange to hear her telling stories about surfing in California.

"Surfing looks scary to me," Meri said at one point. "Sonia must be brave. I would be worried about sharks."

"I said that too." Jasmine nodded. "Sonia told us that one girl had her arm bitten right off by a shark. And that girl still surfed with just one arm."

Meri thought about that. She decided that surfing again after a shark bit off your arm was even harder than trying to apologize for being mean. She decided she'd just have to find another way to apologize.

Saying Good-bye

When recess was over, Mrs. Miller told everyone that she had read their writing practice pages. "You have all done some very hard things," she said. "But one paper was about a hard thing right in our classroom. I am very proud of the writer. I wondered if she'd read it for us?" Mrs. Miller looked right at Meri.

Meri felt her stomach clench. What if reading her paper made Sonia angrier? What if everyone hated Meri then? Mrs. Miller kept smiling her warm smile. Finally Meri stood up and walked over to take the paper.

She turned to face the class. Everyone looked at her curiously, except Gina and

Megan. They nudged each other and whispered.

"Ladies," Mrs. Miller said, looking directly at them, "remember to be quiet and respectful whenever anyone reads." Gina and Megan's faces snapped forward, and they sat very still.

Meri cleared her throat and started reading. "When Room Eight got two new students from California, everyone wanted to be their friends. It's hard for me sometimes to make lots of friends. And I've never lived anywhere cool like California. I guess I was jealous. I didn't think I was, but now I do."

She risked a quick glance up at Jasmine and saw her friend smiling and nodding. Meri locked her eyes back on the paper and kept reading. "I wasn't very nice to Sonia. I said she was a show-off. I don't think she is really. I think I was just mad at how easy it was for everyone to like her. So I wanted to apologize, but it was a lot harder than I thought."

Meri peeked quickly at Sonia to see if she looked mad. Instead, Sonia looked really interested. Meri took a deep breath and kept reading.

"I tried to tell her I was sorry, but she didn't want to talk to me. I guess that was fair. I don't like to talk to mean people either. I don't think I'm a mean person, but I think I acted like one. I tried to write a note telling her I was sorry, but my note got torn up.

"I feel sorry, but it's been really hard to say it. I guess what I learned is that if you do something mean, it's hard to make it better. I learned that I don't want to be a mean girl. And I learned that I wish I'd heard Sonia's California stories."

She lowered the paper. Her face felt hotter than summer sunshine, but her hands felt cold. Mrs. Miller clapped her hands, and most of the kids joined in.

"Thank you for being so honest," Mrs. Miller said.

Sonia's hand shot into the air. Mrs. Miller called on her and Sonia stood. "I forgive you for what you said," Sonia announced. "And I don't think you're a mean girl."

Everyone but Gina and Megan clapped then. Sonia sat back down, but she smiled at Meri in a friendly way. The rest of the school day felt a lot friendlier to Meri. When reading groups were called, David told her that he thought her paper was great.

"You're really brave," David said.

"I was really scared," Meredith admitted. "But I'd be more afraid of sharks."

David looked confused for a second, and then he smiled. "I like sharks. I watch shark shows whenever they come on television. I've even seen the movie *Jaws*, but that shark wasn't real. Hey, can we read a book about sharks next?"

Meri and Jasmine looked at one another, and then they laughed.

"Sure," Meri said. "I guess I can be that brave."

After school, Meri rushed upstairs to talk to Sarah. She dropped her backpack beside the desk and launched right into the way Gina had acted.

"Oh my," Sarah said. "I'm so sorry she tore up your beautiful note. The bird was so pretty. I wish you could have saved it."

"Its head ripped off," Meri said. "And Gina crumpled it. I don't think I could fix it. I could try to draw another sometime."

"So how will you apologize next?"

"I don't have to," Meri said. She told Sarah about the writing practice and how she'd read it out loud in class. "And Sonia said she forgave me. She even smiled at me."

"I am so very glad," Sarah said. "Perhaps you will even be friends. I do wish I could hear some of the stories of California. I am certain I will never go to such a faraway place."

"Well, she hasn't told me any yet," Meri said. "But my friend Jasmine passed along one of her stories. Would you like to hear that?"

Sarah said that she did. Meri told her the surfing story and even the part about the girl who was bitten by a shark. Sarah's eyes grew very wide and round.

"Oh, surely that isn't true!" she whispered. "Her arm was bitten right off?"

Meri nodded. "I'm sure it took her a long time to get well after that. But she still surfs. I'm going to try to find out more about her."

"She is so brave," Sarah said. "I will think about this girl too. When I am very cold and wet, I will look down at both my hands and think how lucky I am. When people push me or scold me, I will think, 'At least you are not a shark.'"

Meri laughed at that. "Maybe I'll try that with Gina and Megan. At least they aren't sharks."

Sarah's face grew serious and she looked at Meri intently. "I believe I am ready to go back to my attic. You have been a wonderful new friend, and this room is so warm and comfortable. Still, I can't help thinking about my secret friend. I was so cold and hungry before. My bed was hard and my blanket was so thin. It was the best magic in the world when I woke up with a warm blanket and hot food right in my room!"

"It must have been terrible," Meri said.

"It was. Sometimes it was even hard to pretend," Sarah said. "But now when I am cold or hungry, I think about the lovely surprises waiting for me in my room."

"I'm so glad," Meri said. "I understand why you miss that."

"You said that you are sure I will learn who it is," Sarah said and Meri nodded. "I do so want him to know how thankful I am to him and how happy he has made me. Anyone who is kind wants to know when people have been made happy. They care for that more than for being thanked."

Meri looked at Sarah sadly. "You will find out, and everything will be wonderful. I'm going to miss you."

"And I will miss you terribly," Sarah said. "But I think you will be well and happy. I will always remember your kindness and your courage to do the right thing. But I need to go."

Meri nodded. "Okay, I'm glad I got to know you. And I'm glad you helped me be more like a princess."

Sarah smiled at her very sweetly as Meri picked up the book from the desk and slipped it back into her backpack. She carried the backpack over to her bed, and then looked back at the mirror. Sarah was already beginning to fade, looking more like a ghost than a girl. Meri waved at her, and Sarah waved back.

Then Meri sat down on the bed and began working on her homework. She didn't want to watch her new friend disappear completely.

"I can always invite her to come back sometimes," Meri whispered with a small sniffle.

10

Sean Had an Idea . . .

The next morning, Meri's stomach felt a little squirmy as she walked into Room Eight. Would Sonia still be nice to her, or would Meri still feel left out of everything? As soon as she came into the room, she ducked into the coatroom. It gave her a moment to take deep breaths, while she hung up her backpack.

She peeked out of the coatroom and saw girls clustered around Sonia's table. Not everyone was in the group, but Meri knew Sonia must be telling a story. Meri crept closer. Sonia looked at her and smiled. Then she waved for Meri to come over.

Meri smiled back and began to weave between the other tables to get close enough to listen. She stopped suddenly when Gina shouted, "You are inviting *her* over?"

"She said she wanted to hear about California," Sonia said. "You heard her paper yesterday."

"She didn't mean that," Gina said. "She was just writing something so Mrs. Miller would like her even more."

"I did mean it," Meri insisted.

"I believe you," Sonia said. She looked down at Kaylin beside her. "Did you believe her?"

Kaylin nodded quickly, though she looked nervously at Gina.

"Well, I didn't," Gina said.

Megan stood up beside Gina. "I don't believe her either. This was our table before Sonia got here. It was our table even before Kaylin started to sit with us. So what we say goes. And we say Meri can't come over here."

Meri froze and looked at Sonia. Would she give in to the two meanest girls in the whole school? Sonia nodded at Gina and Megan calmly. Meri felt her stomach sink.

"You're right," Sonia said. "It's your table. You should have a say about what happens at your table." She stood up and smiled at Meri. "Can I come and sit at your table? I'll tell you about the time I was almost run over by a skateboard train at the beach."

Meri nodded and backed up toward her table. Sonia hopped up and followed her. A few of the other girls followed her too. Halfway across the classroom, Sonia stopped and turned back. She looked right at Kaylin. "Are you coming too?" she asked.

Kaylin looked like the question hurt. Her eyes darted to Gina and Megan, who still stood with their arms crossed. Then Kaylin looked at Sonia. Finally she sighed. "No, I better stay here," she said. Her voice sounded so sad that Meri almost wanted to tell Sonia to go back.

Sonia looked puzzled and a little sad too. But she shrugged. "Okay," she said. "Come on over if you change your mind." Then she looked at Meri. "That would be okay, right? She could come over if she wants?"

"Sure," Meri said.

Kaylin didn't say anything. She just looked down at her hands. Finally, Sonia turned away, and they walked the rest of the way to Meri's table, where Jasmine sat smiling brightly.

"Hi, Jazzy," Sonia said cheerfully.

"Jazzy?" Meri mouthed at her friend.

Jasmine just smiled. "Hi, Sonia. Hi, Meri."

Sonia slipped into the chair across from Jasmine and said, "Okay, it all started one day when Sean and I walked our dog down at the beach. There were these guys skateboarding, and Sean had an idea . . ."

The girls who had followed Sonia over laughed and Jasmine joined in. Meri suspected that "Sean had an idea" must be something they'd heard in Sonia's stories before. Sonia told them how Sean had talked the skateboarders into trying to make a skateboarding chain. They used bungee cords to connect themselves together by belt loops on their shorts.

"It worked great at first," Sonia said. "I was holding my dog's leash. Scout loves to chase kids on bikes. I guess he felt the same way about skateboards. He dragged me right in front of the train. The first guy tried to swerve and fell off his skateboard. This pulled the second guy off the skateboard, and the next guy. And one guy dove off his board, which pulled the shorts down on the guy in front of him."

As she described the pile of skateboards and riders, Meri laughed so hard her stomach hurt. At least this time, it was a good kind of stomachache.

At the end of Sonia's story, Mrs. Miller walked in and began passing out the morning work packets. She smiled and winked at Meri when she saw Sonia sitting at her table. Meri smiled back.

As the morning passed, Meri learned that Sonia was smart and funny. She said math was the only subject that she found hard. "Mostly it's just word problems," she said. "The story parts confuse me. I guess I get distracted by the whole idea of the story."

"I have another friend like that," Meri said. She thought about Sarah wanting to turn story problems into full stories.

After lunch, Mrs. Miller announced that she wanted everyone to head outside for some fresh air. "I know a lot of you girls have been enjoying Sonia's stories," she said. "I think that's great, but you need to go enjoy them outside."

Mrs. Miller called Meri aside before she got to the door.

"Yes?" Meri asked.

"I just wanted to say that I'm proud of how you handled your jealousy," Mrs. Miller said.

"Some girls never really find a way to conquer that."

"I'm glad too," Meri said. "Sonia's really nice. I don't know why I didn't see that right away."

Mrs. Miller smiled. "Well, you see it now and you've found a way to patch things up. I think that's what's important. You know, Sonia really belongs in the same reading group as you. I think she would like that now."

"I'd like that too," Meri said.

"Good," Mrs. Miller said. She stood up and something slipped off the edge of her chair. Mrs. Miller and Meri both jumped in surprise when they saw a snake clinging to her skirt.

Mrs. Miller plucked the snake off and Meri could see it was made of rubber. A paper clip was tied to the snake's head so it could be clipped to Mrs. Miller. "Hmm, looks like Sean likes a good joke."

Meri looked at the floppy snake. "Why do you think it was Sean?" she asked.

Mrs. Miller held up the snake so its pale underbelly showed. Stamped on the rubber were the words *San Diego Zoo*. She looked up at Meri. "What do you think?"

"Is he in trouble?" Meri asked. She didn't like to think of him being in trouble. He seemed nice.

Mrs. Miller shook her head. "No, I didn't mind. No one was hurt or upset. But we'll have to keep an eye out. Pranks rarely happen just once." Then she dropped the snake in the drawer and closed it. "But it's nothing for you to worry about. You should run outside. You might be missing a story."

Meri nodded as she turned toward the door. "I've missed enough of them. I don't plan to miss any more."

About the Author

Jan Fields grew up loving stories where exciting and slightly impossible things happened to ordinary kids like her. She still loves reading stories like that, so she writes books for children looking for the same things.

When she's not writing, Jan pokes around the New England countryside in search of inspiration, magic mirrors, and fairies.